*Every new generation of children is enthralled by the famous stories in our Well-loved Tales series. Younger ones love to have the story read to them. Older children will enjoy the exciting stories in an easy-to-read text.*

Published by Ladybird Books Ltd  Loughborough  Leicestershire  UK
Ladybird Books Inc  Lewiston  Maine 04240  USA

# The Little Mermaid

retold for easy reading
by ENID C KING

illustrated by BRIAN PRICE THOMAS

Ladybird Books

4

# THE LITTLE MERMAID

Far away in the deep, deep sea there was a place where the water was blue and crystal clear.

In the deepest part stood the palace of the Mer-king. It had coral walls, tall amber windows and a roof made of shells. The Mer-king lived there with six lovely daughters and their grandmother. The youngest of them had sea-blue eyes and delicate skin. Like all mermaids, she had no legs. Instead she had a tail like a fish.

Some of the princesses collected things that had fallen from passing ships to decorate their gardens.

The youngest princess chose just to grow red flowers and a single red tree. In the middle of her garden was a statue of a young boy. Simple things pleased her, for she was a strange, quiet child.

Most of all she enjoyed hearing about the world above the sea. She would ask her grandmother again and again to tell her about men and ships and animals. She liked to hear about flowers you could smell and creatures called birds that flew through the trees.

"When you are fifteen, you can rise to the surface of the sea and see all these things for yourself," said her grandmother.

It would be a year before her oldest sister became fifteen. Each sister was a year older than the next, so it would be six whole years before the youngest would see the world above the water. The oldest sister promised to tell them all she had seen when her turn came.

Sometimes at night the youngest princess would look up through the clear blue water. She could see the pale glow of the stars and the moon. Sometimes a large shadow passed overhead and she knew this must be either a whale or a ship. She liked to imagine it was a ship, full of the strange beings who lived above the waves. She wished she could see them for herself.

At last the day came when the oldest princess could rise to the surface of the sea. All her sisters waited eagerly for her to come back. Then they listened while she told them of a town near the coast.

"There were hundreds of lights," she said, "and music and the sound of bells from tall church towers."

The youngest princess was even more impatient. The next year the second daughter had her turn. She came back and talked about a vivid sunset, with clouds of gold and red and violet. She had seen a flock of birds fly overhead and described how beautiful they looked. The youngest daughter wished so hard for her turn to come.

When the third princess became fifteen she was very brave and swam up a great river. She had seen the hills and the trees and the houses and castles. She told of the sun that was hot on her face and the children that swam in the water, although they had no tails.

The fourth sister did not go so far. She could only talk of the ships sailing by and the whales spouting water. Her sister, the fifth princess, saw many different things. It was winter when she rose to the surface. She talked about icebergs and storms and huge black clouds. She told of the blue flashes of lightning that zigzagged across

the sea and of the great rolls of thunder that followed.

After a time, the five sisters grew tired of their journey to the surface. They liked to stay at home in the palace. Sometimes, however, they all rose together, hand in hand, and sang in their sweet voices to the sailors on the ships. The sailors thought it was the sound of the wind and took no notice. The youngest mermaid sat in her father's palace and wished even harder for her turn to come.

At long last, the great day came. Her grandmother tidied her hair and put her crown on her head. She rose up and up until her head was above the surface.

The sun had just set. There was no wind and the sea was smooth. A large ship lay still on the water, all her lamps glowing against the dark sky. Music and singing were coming from the ship.

The little mermaid swam close. When a wave

lifted her she could see into the cabin. A party was going on. It was the prince's birthday and all the men on board were enjoying themselves. The prince was a handsome young man. When he came on deck they set off hundreds of fireworks and the little mermaid was frightened. She dived under the water but soon came back to the surface. She wanted to see the handsome prince again.

While she waited and watched, a storm blew
up. The waves grew higher and higher. The wind
howled and the ship was tossed about like a toy
boat. Suddenly a great gust of wind turned the
ship over. The water rushed in and broke it in

pieces. The sea was full of wood and broken
pieces from the ship. The little mermaid searched
for the prince in the darkness. She was afraid he
had drowned when the ship sank. She knew that
humans could not live under water as she could.

A flash of lightning showed her where the
prince was. He was almost drowned and he was
too tired to swim any more. She took hold of him
and kept his head above the waves.

When morning came the prince still had his eyes closed. The little mermaid looked round and saw the seashore not far away. There was a bay with smooth dry sand. She took the prince there and laid him in the warm sun. There was a building nearby with bells ringing from it. The little mermaid swam out to sea and waited.

Some of the people from the convent came out and found the prince. They were worried because they thought he was dead. Soon, the prince got better and the people were glad. They took him into a house and the little mermaid was sad. The prince would never know who had saved him. She was so sad that she dived below the waves and went to her father's palace.

Her sisters asked her what she had seen. She only told them about a ship and a house and said no more. Often she rose to the surface and swam to the bay where she had left the prince. She hoped to see him but he was never there. Sadly, she went back to her garden and the statue. It was like the prince and she often put her arms round it.

She was so sad that, at last, she had to tell one of her sisters the whole story; all about the storm, the shipwreck and the handsome prince. One of the young mermaids knew who he was and where he lived.

Together, all the princesses swam up to the palace where the prince lived. It was a very fine building with tall clear windows and statues that looked almost real. Inside you could see beautiful rooms with silk curtains and many pictures.

Now that the little mermaid knew where the prince lived, she went there often. She was very brave and swam close to the land to watch the prince. Sometimes he sailed in a small boat. Sometimes she would hear the fishermen talking about him. She was happy to think that she had saved him.

When she saw all the human beings in the palace, she wished she was one of them. There were so many things they could do. She asked her sisters lots of questions, but they didn't know the

answers. She had to ask her grandmother who knew all about the world above the sea.

"Do men live for ever, if they are not drowned?" asked the princess.

"No, they die, just as we die. But their life is much shorter than ours. We live to be three hundred years old. But when we die we just become foam on the sea. Humans have souls, and when they die their souls go to live in a wonderful country far away," said her grandmother.

"I think I would rather be a human, just for one day," said the little mermaid. "I would happily give up my three hundred years if I could have a soul, like the humans."

"Is there no way I can get a soul, dear grandmother?" asked the princess, sadly.

"Only if a human begins to love you," said her grandmother. "But that won't happen. Human beings do not like our tails. They have two things called legs, which they think are better."

This made the little princess sad. Even a wonderful court ball didn't cheer her up. Half way through, she went to sit in her favourite garden, feeling sorry for herself. Above her she could see ships moving. This made her think even more about the handsome prince.

"I must do something," she said to herself. "I know, I'll go and see the witch, while my sisters are busy dancing."

She knew where the witch lived, but had never been there before. It was a terrible journey. First she had to pass through a fierce whirlpool. Then came a slimy bog. The witch's house was in a wood beyond the bog. All the trees had long slimy arms. When anything went past, they stretched out and caught it. She nearly turned back, but then she thought of the prince again and this gave her courage. Twisting her long hair round her head, she swam swiftly until she came to the house.

The house was made of bones. Ugly, fat, yellow snails crawled around. The witch sat stroking a large toad.

"I know what you have come for," said the witch. "You want legs like the humans, instead of your beautiful tail. You are foolish, but you can have your wish. You hope that with legs the handsome prince will begin to love you."

The witch laughed so much the toad fell off her lap. "I will tell you what you must do. You must take a magic drink and swim to the surface. Sit on the rocks and drink it. Your tail will split in two and turn into legs. It will be very painful. If you think you can stand the pain I will help you."

"Oh yes, I'm sure I can," said the little mermaid, thinking of the handsome prince.

"Remember," said the witch, "once you turn into a human you can never turn back again. If the prince doesn't marry you, you will never get a human soul. The day he marries someone else you will die. You will become foam on the sea, like other mermaids."

"I still want to try it," said the little mermaid.

"One other thing," said the witch, "you must pay me for the magic drink. I want the best thing you own."

"What is that?" asked the mermaid.

"Your voice," said the witch.

"But if I have no voice, how will I win the prince?"

"You will have to use your grace and charm and your beautiful eyes," said the witch.

The little mermaid loved the prince so much.

Sadly she agreed to give away her voice. The witch set up her cauldron and it boiled and bubbled. When the magic drink was ready it was crystal clear.

"Here it is," said the witch handing her the bottle. At that moment the little mermaid became dumb. She swam back through the horrid wood. No one tried to stop her. They were all afraid of the magic drink in her hand.

When she came to her father's palace, all the lights were out. Everyone was asleep. She wanted to go and say goodbye but she couldn't. She was dumb.

She picked a flower from each of her sisters' gardens. She took them to remind her of her home and family. Turning away quickly, she swam to where the prince lived.

It was still dark when she got there. She sat on the marble staircase and drank the magic liquid. She felt a sharp pain and then she fainted. When she woke up it was morning.

She looked down and saw that her tail

had become two slim legs. Standing looking at her was the handsome prince. He asked who she was and how she got there, but she could only smile at him.

He led her into the palace. There they found her some beautiful clothes to wear. Everyone said how gracefully she walked, but the little mermaid was sad because she couldn't talk.

When a young servant girl sang she was even sadder. She knew she used to have a voice far sweeter than that.

But when the servant girls danced, she joined in. She danced better than any of them. She was so light and graceful, everyone stopped to watch her. The prince, especially, was enchanted. He said she must always stay with him. She slept in a nearby room. She went with him when he rode on horseback. She walked with him in the mountains. But all the time her feet hurt her, as the witch had told her they would.

At night time, when everyone was asleep, she crept out of the palace. She went down the steps to bathe her feet in the sea. She looked into the water and remembered her family far below.

One evening her sisters came to the steps and she waved to them. They told her how sad she had made them.

Every morning they came to see her. Once they brought her grandmother. Another time they brought her father. They all stretched out their arms to her, but they never spoke.

The prince grew very fond of the little mermaid. He thought she was beautiful, but he did not ask her to be his wife.

One day he said to her,

"You remind me of a girl I saw once. My ship was wrecked in a storm. When I woke up, a girl had helped me to the shore. She had saved my life. I shall never forget her, but she is the only person I could love. I am so happy that you remind me of her."

The little mermaid was very sad. "He doesn't know that I saved him and took him to the shore. He thinks it was one of the girls from the convent. He thinks they do not marry and that he will not meet her again."

One day the little mermaid heard that the prince was going on a journey. He was going to see a princess in another country.

"My parents hope I will marry her," said the prince. "But she cannot look like the girl who

saved me. I love her and you remind me of her. If I have to marry anyone else I would rather marry you."

This made the little mermaid very sad, but she could say nothing. She could not tell the prince the truth. She had given away her voice.

They travelled on a ship to the other country. Each night when everyone was asleep, her sisters swam up to see her. She waved and smiled to them. She could not tell them that she was happy with her prince.

Next day they arrived at the city. The church bells rang. There were processions in the street. But the princess had not arrived. She had been at a convent far away, to learn how to be a princess. When she came, she was very beautiful.

When the prince saw her he was amazed.
"You are the girl who saved my life," he said.
He turned to the little mermaid and said,

"I did not dare to hope that I would see this
girl again. You must be happy too, for you have
always loved me more than anyone else."

The little mermaid thought her heart would break. She knew that the day the prince got married, she would die. But she had to pretend to be happy.

All the preparations for the wedding went on. At the wedding, she walked behind the princess and carried her train. That night they all went on board the ship. There was a special tent in the middle of the deck for the prince and princess. It had soft beds and lovely silk curtains.

When it was dark, all the coloured lamps were lit. Everyone danced. It looked just like the party the mermaid had seen so long ago. When everyone had gone to bed, the little mermaid leaned on the ship's rail. She looked at the sky. When the sun rose, she knew that she would die.

Suddenly her sisters appeared. They looked very pale and their long hair had gone.

"We gave our hair to the witch to use for magic," they said. "She has given us this sharp knife. If you use it to kill the prince, you will become a mermaid again. Hurry, before the sun rises."

The little mermaid took the knife.
She went into the tent where the prince
was asleep. She looked down at
him, but she could not kill him.
Instead, she took the
knife and threw it.

It fell into the sea and the waves blazed with colour where it landed. She took one last look at the prince. Then she threw herself into the sea. Slowly she turned into foam.

As the sun rose she felt its warmth. She heard sweet voices and could see strange lights in the sky. She felt herself being lifted and soon she was in the sky with all the lights round her.

"Where are you taking me?" she asked.

"To join the daughters of the air," they said. "Mermaids do not have souls, and neither do the daughters of the air. But we can earn our souls by the good deeds we do.

"We send cool breezes to hot countries to refresh the children. We spread the scent of flowers for everyone to enjoy. We try to help anyone who suffers. If you help us, in three hundred years you may have a soul."

49

On the ship, the prince and princess were sad. They could not find the beautiful girl who could not speak. They looked at the sea as though they knew where she had gone. They could not see the little mermaid, smiling at them as she drifted past behind a cloud.